GREAT ESCAPES

SURVIVAL IN THE WILDERNESS

Great Escapes
Nazi Prison Camp Escape
Journey to Freedom, 1838
Civil War Breakout

GREAT ESCAPES

SURVIVAL IN THE WILDERNESS

BY **STEVEN OTFINOSKI**

EDITED BY **MICHAEL TEITELBAUM**

HARPER

An Imprint of HarperCollinsPublishers

To Beverly,
who I couldn't survive without

ISBN 978-0-06-286045-3 (trade bdg.)

ISBN 978-0-06-286044-6 (pbk.)

20 21 22 23 24 PC/BRR 10 9 8 7 6 5 4 3 2 1

First Edition

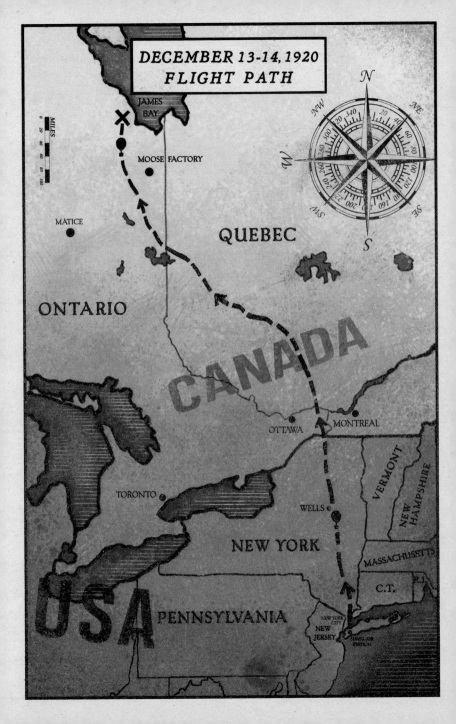

DECEMBER 13-14, 1920
FLIGHT PATH

PROLOGUE

It was now or never. The young man reached for the cord connected to the gas valve. He gave it a sharp tug and listened as the helium in the balloon rushed out with a loud hiss.

The balloon plunged toward the earth.

The young man's cold hands gripped the edge of the basket, holding on for dear life as it crashed into a vast blanket of fir and pine trees.

The balloon bumped and knocked against branches and trunks, throwing him to the floor of the basket. Pine needles and bits of evergreen sprayed down onto his head and shoulders. As the basket slipped between the trees, the deflated

gas bag became caught in a tangle of tree limbs. Finally the basket landed with a loud thud on the hard ground, tilting over and coming to an abrupt stop on its side. His heart pounding and his legs trembling, the young man clambered out. His two traveling companions followed, visibly shaken, but to his great relief, very much alive.

Together they looked around in bewilderment at a world of white. They stood alone in a desolate land of snow and ice and tall trees as far as the eye could see. All they had were the clothes on their backs and the meager contents of the balloon: a compass, a box of matches, two packs of cigarettes, a penknife, and a cage of cooing carrier pigeons. How had they ended up in the middle of this vast wilderness? The young man knew they were more than a thousand miles from home and felt a chill work its way into his bones.

How are we going to get out of this alive?

Chapter One

A FATEFUL DECISION

Monday, December 13, 1920

"Beautiful view from up here," murmured navy lieutenant Walter Hinton as he looked down from the wicker basket that hung beneath the gas balloon. "But it's a long way down!"

Two thousand feet below lay the Brooklyn Navy Yard. The ships just off the coast looked like toys in a bathtub. Hinton gazed in wonder at small buildings, tiny roads, and people the size of ants. The entire world stretched out in miniature beneath him.

"Don't lean so far over the side," cautioned Lieutenant Louis Kloor, only half seriously. "We wouldn't want to lose you this early in our flight."

Kloor, the leader of this training flight across New York state, smiled. At age twenty-two he was ten years younger than Hinton and young enough to be the son of forty-five-year-old Lieutenant Stephen Farrell, the third member of their team. Hinton and Farrell, both good friends of Kloor's, were on board because the navy wanted all its officers to have some balloon experience. The two older men called blue-eyed, smooth-faced Kloor "the Kid," but despite his youth, Kloor was a seasoned ballooning veteran.

THREE MEN OF ACTION

Hinton and Farrell may not have been experienced balloonists, but they were veteran airplane pilots.

Hinton grew up on a farm in Ohio and joined the navy as a young man. In May 1919, he was one of two pilots in a six-man crew that flew the NC-4, a pioneering four-engine airplane, across the Atlantic Ocean. The NC-4 was the only one of the three airplanes in the flight to succeed. The other two were forced to land in the ocean due to poor visibility. But Hinton's NC-4 carried on, arriving in Lisbon, Portugal, after a nineteen-day flight. They were the first aviators to cross the Atlantic, eight years before Charles Lindbergh's celebrated transatlantic solo flight. Hinton was awarded the Navy Cross and a Congressional Gold Medal for his achievement.

Farrell was born near Oswego, New York, and enlisted in the navy in 1896. In World War I he was an armament officer at a US naval air station in England. In his younger days, Farrell was a first-class boxer and attained the title of heavyweight champion of the Pacific Fleet, a title he defended for years. Now, at age forty-five, he weighed two hundred pounds and struggled to keep his weight down with exercise and diet.

Kloor, despite his youth, had his own list of achievements. A native of Louisiana, he was one of the youngest aviators in the US Navy and had already flown ten balloon trips. He'd also seen his share of danger. In July 1920, only five months before his flight with Hinton and Farrell, Kloor had survived a crash over Jamaica Bay, New York, when his navy dirigible, a gas-filled airship, crashed into the sea. Kloor was aware of the risks of flying, but on the morning of December 13 he had no reason to believe the training flight across New York state would be anything but routine.

About two hours into the flight from the Rockaway Naval Air Station at the westward end of Long Island, Kloor took out a sheet of paper and began writing.

"What are you doing?" Farrell asked.

"I'm writing down our coordinates for the naval officials back at Rockaway, to let them know our position," he explained. Then he opened the birdcage attached to the rigging. Carefully he lifted out one of the four carrier pigeons with both hands. He attached the note to the bird's leg and gently let it go. The pigeon flapped its wings and took off for home.

"Smart bird," said Hinton.

"The smartest," agreed Kloor. "It'll get our

message back to the station."

Lieutenant Farrell looked at the bird as it slowly grew smaller, until it became no more than a dot in the sea of sky. Then he stared down at the earth far below. He was both fascinated by and fearful of the balloon.

Unlike an airplane, it had no engine and no mechanism to steer. It was the hydrogen gas that allowed it to soar in the skies. The pilot could only control it going up or down. To go up, he had to pour out sand from one of the twenty-one thirty-pound sandbags in the basket, lightening the load. This was the ballast. To descend, the pilot opened a valve to release some of the hydrogen gas.

CARRIER PIGEONS

For more than three thousand years, carrier pigeons have been able to find their homes over long distances, using "compass sense," which allows the birds to orient themselves by the sun, allowing them to deliver written messages. The ancient Egyptians were among the first people to keep carrier pigeons.

In 1860, newsman Paul Reuter, who would go on to start a news wire service, developed a fleet of forty-five pigeons to deliver news and stock reports between Brussels, Belgium, and Aachen, Germany.

Carrier pigeons were also used in World War I to deliver messages. One particularly heroic French pigeon, named Cher Ami, was awarded the Croix de Guerre (War Cross) for delivering twelve important messages. On his final mission, he survived being shot through the breast and leg.

The United States Signal Corps also used carrier pigeons to send messages in World War II (1939–45) and in the Korean War (1950–53).

Today, carrier pigeons, more often called homing pigeons, are mostly kept for racing. The birds are let go at a release point by each owner. The bird arriving back home in the fastest time is the winner. However, in a remote part of eastern India, police were using pigeons to communicate with victims of natural disasters as late as 2002.

The three men passed a pleasant afternoon in comfortable chairs in the balloon's basket as they crossed the state of New York in a northerly direction. Although it was cold, they stayed warm in their bulky flight suits, which were lined with silk, insulated with a layer of fleece, and overlaid with a tightly woven, weatherproof cotton.

"Sorry to be so last-minute in inviting you on the flight," said Kloor as he bit into one of the eight sandwiches they had packed.

"It's all right," said Farrell, sipping hot coffee from a thermos bottle. "I needed to get away and get my mind off Sis."

"I didn't know you had a sister," said Hinton.

"Oh, no," laughed Farrell. "Sis is what we call my daughter, Emily. She's ill at home in New Jersey with scarlet fever. But I hope to cheer her up with stories about our balloon adventure when we get back."

The night slowly descended like a thick curtain and they gazed up as the stars began to appear in the darkened sky, sparkling like salt crystals.

"It's beautiful," murmured Farrell. "Thanks

again for inviting me along."

"You would have had to go up sooner or later," Kloor said to Farrell.

"Well, I'm glad it's sooner rather than later," said Hinton, taking another sip of the hot coffee. It warmed his body as the night air grew colder.

"What's that down there?" asked Kloor, scanning the ground below. "Looks like a light coming from a house."

"You've got a good pair of eyes," said Farrell, squinting into the darkness. "I never would have spotted it."

"Well, gentlemen," said Kloor, "I think it's time we found out what our position is."

He opened the valve and released some of the gas. The balloon began a slow descent through the deepening darkness. Suddenly, the drag rope trailing outside the balloon pulled tight, getting caught in a tangle of tree branches. The balloon came to a stop about a hundred feet from the ground.

"Not to worry," said Kloor calmly. "We can get the rope untangled once we find out where we are."

Through the trees, they saw the house again,

more clearly now. A man emerged from within.

"Excuse me, sir!" Kloor yelled down to him. "Can you tell us where we are?"

The man was startled by the balloon hovering above his home, but soon regained his composure. "You're near the town of Wells," he cried. "In the Adirondacks."

"And how far are we from Albany?" asked Kloor, referring to the state capital.

The man raised one arm and pointed to the southeast. "About sixty miles thataway," he said.

Kloor thanked him and turned to his two companions. "Well, gentlemen, if you've had enough, this could be the end of our voyage. We could land the balloon safely right here, walk into town, and make our way home in the morning," he told them.

Farrell and Hinton exchanged looks.

"Is that normal for a training flight?" Hinton asked.

"Well, no," replied Kloor. "They normally last a full twenty-four hours, meaning we would be landing tomorrow."

"Then I'm for going on," said Hinton.

"I agree," said Farrell. "I've never spent a night in a balloon."

"You've never spent *any* time in a balloon," said Hinton with a laugh. "I haven't either. And so far this has been a great adventure. So let's get on with it."

Kloor was delighted with their decision. With the assistance of his companions, he untangled the drag rope and pulled it free. The balloon began to rise again into the inky night sky.

Chapter Two

A STORMY NIGHT

As the balloon rose over the treetops of northern New York state, the men settled back to enjoy the cool evening breeze and gaze at the constellation of lights below as they passed over towns and villages. Then Farrell felt the first drop on his head. And another.

"I think it's starting to rain," he said.

While the balloon tethered above kept most of the rain off them, some of it dripped down into the basket.

"I didn't see any rain in the forecast," Kloor said. "But we're upstate now and the weather can be changeable here."

There was a rumble of thunder and the wind began to pick up, tousling their hair.

"Looks like we're in for a storm," said Farrell, trying to sound calm as the rain began to fall in earnest.

Hinton grabbed the remaining sandwiches and shoved them under a chair.

"We're getting soaked," said Farrell.

"That's not our main worry," said Kloor, staring up at the gas valve. "It's the wind. I'm concerned it could throw us off course and—"

But his words were cut short by a gust of air that almost jolted them off their feet. Hinton grabbed the edge of the basket and looked around. The drag rope was again coming dangerously close to the treetops.

"We've got to land!" cried Hinton above the shrieking sound of the wind.

"We can't land here," Kloor shouted over the wind's roar. "There's no town or house in sight. We'd be completely stranded. We've got to stay aloft and get rid of the ballast."

"What do you mean?" asked Farrell.

"The sandbags!" cried Kloor. "We've got to dump them over the side, so the balloon rises and clears the trees. Hurry!"

Hinton and Farrell began untying the sandbags, one by one, and dumping them overboard at Kloor's direction. At first it didn't seem to make any difference, but then, all at once the balloon began to ascend into the stormy sky.

"Thank God!" cried Farrell. "I thought we were goners!"

"We're not out of danger yet," cautioned Kloor. "Let's hope the wind dies down soon and we can stabilize our flight pattern."

Hinton looked up at the balloon bag. "Is it my imagination or has the balloon shrunk?" he asked.

Kloor gazed up and grimaced. The balloon was beginning to descend again. "It's not your imagination," he said. "It must be the gas in the bag. It's at least ten days old and is losing its strength."

"Didn't you know that before we left Rockaway?" asked Farrell in exasperation.

"I was told that it wouldn't be a problem for our short flight," replied Kloor.

"Well, it's clear that whoever told you that was wrong. And now we're in big trouble," Farrell said.

"Settle down, Steve," said Hinton. "Arguing among ourselves isn't going to solve anything." Then he turned to Kloor. "What's the plan?" he asked.

"Get rid of the rest of the ballast to keep the balloon aloft," said Kloor. "If we keep descending we'll crash for sure."

"There are only a few sandbags left," said Farrell.

"Then we'll have to throw over the drag rope and anything else that's weighing us down," said Kloor.

While Farrell threw over the last sandbags, Kloor and Hinton hauled in the heavy drag rope, which resembled a thick, long snake. Kloor took Farrell's penknife and began cutting the rope.

"What are you doing?" Hinton asked him.

"Cutting the rope into smaller pieces. We'll heave them over the side one by one as needed."

But even after all ten pieces had been thrown over the side, the balloon still hung dangerously close to the treetops.

"What do we do now?" cried Farrell.

"Tear up the carpet," said Kloor.

They did, and heaved it over the side, too. The balloon still refused to rise.

"We're going down," said Farrell, his voice trembling. "We won't get out of this alive."

Kloor began ripping out the lining of the basket. "The seats! Throw out the seats!"

Hinton and Farrell tossed the seats into the clouded air. *This is it,* thought Hinton. *There's nothing more we can do to lighten the balloon except to throw each other overboard.*

But at that very moment the balloon started to lift. It slowly rose above the trees, higher and higher.

"We're going up!" cried Farrell. "We're clearing the trees!"

"We're going to make it!" yelled Hinton.

The men cheered and embraced each other. The Kid had saved them after all!

The wind eventually let up, and they continued floating above the tree line. But the rain kept pounding down, soaking them to the skin.

"Look!" cried Farrell, pointing at a glow of bright lights below. "It looks like we're passing over a city."

"Where do you think we are?" Hinton asked Kloor.

"I'm not sure," said Kloor, trying to remain calm and in control of a situation he actually had little control over.

"What difference does it matter what city it is?" reasoned Hinton. "Can't we land here somewhere?"

Kloor shook his head. "No. Not while it's dark and stormy and we can't see the ground. It's too dangerous. We'll have to wait until it's light."

"If you'd thought to bring a map maybe we could figure out where we are," said Farrell. "You're supposed to be the expert balloonist, aren't you?"

Kloor had no answer. He relied on experience and instinct, and both were failing him now. Hinton stared at him, but said nothing. Somehow, his silence made Kloor feel worse than Farrell's accusations.

More time passed and the first rays of dawn

broke through the darkness, revealing a thick layer of fog. While the growing light brought new hope to the men, they couldn't tell what lay below.

"We can't land in a fog like this," admitted Kloor.

The rain stopped, and Hinton looked at his wristwatch. It was nine a.m. As the men stared anxiously at the sky, the sun began to emerge from behind the clouds. Soon its warmth filled them with a renewed spirit, and it proved to be a double blessing. The sun's heat caused the gas in the balloon to expand, raising the balloon higher into the sky.

They continued on their wayward journey for a few more hours, and at about one thirty that afternoon, Kloor spotted something that lifted his spirits.

"Look, down below!" he cried. "I think I see a house!"

"I don't see anything," said Farrell, peering down at the distant ground.

"Neither do I," said Hinton.

"We've passed it," said Kloor excitedly. "But it was a house. I'm sure of it!"

Just then they all heard a sound from below.

"It sounds like a dog barking," said Hinton. "Where there's a dog, there are people."

"We've got to land this thing," said Farrell.

"It's now or never," said Kloor as he reached for the cord connected to the gas valve. He gave it a sharp tug and listened as the gas in the balloon rushed out with a loud hiss. The balloon plunged toward the earth.

BALLOONING

People first took to the skies not in airplanes, but balloons. The Montgolfier brothers, two French papermakers, launched the first successful hot-air balloon flight carrying a sheep, a duck, and a rooster in September 1783 at Versailles, the palace of the French king Louis XVI, who witnessed the flight. The flight lasted eight minutes, covered 2 miles (3.2 km), and the balloon reached a height of 3,000 feet (1,000 m) before landing safely. The balloon consisted of a bag made of silk and paper that contained hot air, and a basket below it for the passengers to ride in. A burner below the balloon bag was fueled by straw, chopped wool, and dried horse manure, and provided the heat that made the balloon rise. The balloon would descend when the air in the bag was allowed to cool. A month later, the Montgolfiers launched the first balloon with three human passengers in Paris.

The other kind of balloon developed around this time was the gas balloon. This balloon was filled with a light gas, such as helium or hydrogen, that lifted it into the air. No heat source was needed. The balloon could be made to ascend by releasing ballast—bags of sand or water— from the basket.

The first successful balloon flight in the United States was launched from a prison yard in Philadelphia in January 1793. President George Washington witnessed the takeoff. The balloon landed safely in New Jersey.

Military balloons were used to observe enemy troop movements on both sides in the Civil War (1861–65) and in World War I. Britain used balloon barrages, balloons from which steel cables were suspended, for protection from low-flying enemy planes. These planes were forced to fly above the balloons to avoid being damaged by the cables. After World War I, in the 1920s, the navy used balloons for observing and recording atmospheric and weather conditions, which is what Kloor would have been doing on longer balloon flights.

Today, ballooning is mostly confined to meteorological and recreational use.

Chapter Three

CRASH LANDING!

The balloon began its rapid descent into the trees below. The basket and the balloon went their separate ways—the balloon trapped in the trees and the basket falling earthward. The men clung to the basket's side as it hit the ground hard and then slid a short distance before coming to rest against a fir tree. The three stumbled out onto the snow-covered landscape.

"Nothing seems broken," said Hinton, feeling his arms and legs. "Are you all right, Steve?"

"Just a bit shook up, but okay," replied Farrell.

"That makes three of us," said Kloor.

They looked around them at a wilderness of

forestland. The ground was covered in snow that crunched under their shoes.

Kloor could see his breath, a tiny cloud of white, puff out from his mouth. Farrell shivered uncontrollably in his wet clothes.

"Good Lord," said Hinton in a hoarse whisper. "Where are we?"

"Wherever we are, we're in a jam," muttered Farrell.

"There's got to be a settlement nearby," said Kloor. "We saw a house."

"*You* saw a house," corrected Farrell.

"But we all heard the dog barking," said Hinton.

He pointed to the southeast. "It was coming from that direction if I'm not mistaken."

"But what if it wasn't a dog?" reasoned Farrell. "It could have been a wild animal. A wolf." His words hung in the silence.

"Let's not let our imaginations run away with us," cautioned Hinton. "If we're going to get out of this mess we've got to keep our heads."

The two other men agreed. Slowly they began to pick through the contents of the ruined basket, gathering what supplies they thought they could make use of. The basket looked pathetically small, much smaller and more cramped than it had when they were riding carelessly in it through the sky. Hinton grabbed the compass, two packs of cigarettes, and a box of table matches. Farrell picked up his overnight bag and felt the penknife in his pocket. He found a certain comfort in the feel of its hard metal in his hand. Kloor removed the cage that contained the three remaining pigeons. "We can send the birds out for help if we need to," he said.

"Or we can eat them," said Hinton. "We've eaten

all the sandwiches and there's nothing else for food. And the coffee's gone and there's no water. Why didn't we think to bring water?"

Kloor and Farrell had no answer to his question. The men cast one last look at the balloon hanging limply in the branches above and headed through the trees in the direction that they had heard the barking dog.

Chapter Four

THE FIRST NIGHT

The men trudged through the forest for several miles, using the compass to lead them in a southeasterly direction.

The terrain was mostly flat, hardened snow only a few inches deep, but it was icy in spots. Hinton and Farrell followed behind Kloor, stepping into his shoe prints so they wouldn't have to exert enough energy to break through the snow with their own feet. Within little more than an hour of walking they were exhausted. They were panting now, mouths open, steaming breath shooting out with each exhale. Another hour passed. The light was beginning to fade and the sun sank behind the trees. They found no house, nor the dog they thought they had heard. Not seeing a trace of civilization, they knew they were alone, lost in a vast wilderness that seemed to have no end.

"We'll make camp here for the night," said Kloor.

Hinton agreed. Farrell, out of breath, merely grunted.

They gathered rotten tree stumps and fallen trunks for firewood in the growing twilight. Using Farrell's penknife and their bare hands, they broke up the wood as best they could. Hinton lit the fire with one match, a feat the two other men appreciated. They had only a dozen matches in the box and knew their survival depended on every single one of them.

They held balls of snow in their hands above the fire. As the snow melted, they drank it. Then Kloor and Farrell settled down around the crackling fire. Suddenly Hinton stood up.

"Where are you going?" asked Kloor.

"To look for running water before it gets any darker," Hinton replied. "If there's a creek nearby it could empty into a river. And people build homes and settlements along rivers."

Kloor was impressed by Hinton's initiative. This was just the kind of man he'd want along in a fix like this. Kloor wasn't so sure about Farrell. The older man already showed signs of breaking down physically. He'd have to keep a close eye on him.

As Hinton tramped through the underbrush, he felt the cold wind slap his face and heard the crunching of his shoes in the hardened snow. His heavy flight suit felt bulky and uncomfortable and he stopped to take it off. He placed the suit on the ground and told himself he'd retrieve it on the way back to camp. Hinton continued on until nearly all the light had bled from the sky, but found no sign of a creek or stream. *We'll keep looking tomorrow,* he told himself. *Surely there's got to be a waterway somewhere.* He turned and started retracing his steps to the camp. In the growing darkness, though, he couldn't find the spot where he'd left his flight suit.

What a fool I was to take it off, he thought to himself. *It was my best protection from the cold. Now I'll freeze half to death.*

He was still furious with himself when he returned to camp. Seeing how badly he felt, Kloor and Farrell said little about the flight suit, not wanting to make him feel even worse.

"Should we kill the pigeons?" said Farrell. "I'm getting hungry."

"No," said Kloor flatly. "Let's wait until tomorrow. We don't know how long we'll have to go without other food."

"The Kid's right," said Hinton. "Best to go hungry tonight and have something to eat tomorrow."

"All right," said Farrell reluctantly. "We'd better bed down then. You can't feel hunger when you're sleeping."

They lay down on pine tree boughs to stay dry and tried to sleep. Kloor curled up by the fire. Farrell and Hinton stayed close together for warmth. Farrell tried to protect and warm Hinton, who no longer had his flight suit, but it was useless. The bitter chill spread through their bodies like a virus. They lay awake all night, listening to the wind, lost in dark thoughts of what lay ahead of them.

The three men arose to a cold dawn. They

threw more wood onto the fire and together eyed the pigeons in their cage.

"I think it's time to eat them," said Farrell, licking his lips. "We've got no other food and I'm starving."

"So am I," said Kloor. "But if we kill them we'll have no way of sending messages for help."

"What good will that do if we starve to death in the meantime?" countered Farrell. "I say we eat them now."

"Hold on," reasoned Hinton. "We're all hungry but we can't eat them all at once. Who knows how long we'll have to live on pigeon meat? I say kill and eat only one of them now."

"That means a mouthful or two at most for each of us," complained Farrell. "That won't fill our stomachs."

"It'll have to do," said Kloor. "We've got to make them last as long as possible."

Farrell made no further fuss and agreed to do the grisly work of killing one of the pigeons by twisting its neck. Kloor plucked the feathers and Hinton roasted the carcass over the open fire.

Once the bird was cooked, each man ate a mouthful or two of pigeon meat. They all felt guilty. After all, these intelligent birds were meant for better things than being eaten for breakfast. But the men's stomachs overruled their consciences.

After finishing the meager meal, they prepared to melt more snow for water. Suddenly, Hinton pointed to a hole in the ground.

"Look!" he cried. "This hole in the earth is filled with water."

"Do you think it's safe to drink?" asked Farrell.

"I don't see why not," reasoned Kloor. "It should be as fresh as the water from the snow."

Hinton cupped his hands and brought some of the water to his lips.

"It tastes a bit brackish, but it's not bad," he said.

The men took turns drinking, grateful that water, at least, would not be one of their concerns. They all knew that dehydration could kill them faster than starvation.

MOOSE LICKS

The holes containing water the men found are called moose licks or mineral licks and are caused by either mineral springs or swamps. Moose and other animals gather to drink at the licks. In many parts of Canada, where (unbeknownst to them) the men were, hunters will also gather at the licks to find moose. Some licks have been around for generations, but in years of severe drought, the licks dry up and disappear.

With breakfast over, the men broke camp and headed east, Hinton taking the lead. Half an hour later, Hinton stopped abruptly. For the first time since the barking dog, he heard something beneath the sound of the wind. It was a soft but persistent murmur. As he moved forward the sound gradually became louder, vying with the rush of wind for his attention.

"Where are you running to?" gasped Farrell, rushing after Hinton.

"Don't you hear it?" Hinton cried.

"Yes!" exclaimed Kloor. "I hear it too! Come on!"

The three ran clumsily onward. Hinton got to it first. He looked at the blue stream beneath his feet and turned back to the others, grinning. "A creek!" he cried.

Chapter Five

DESPERATE MEASURES

Kloor and Farrell caught up to Hinton and they cried for joy at the marvelous sight of the running water, rushing clean and pure over a bed of stone.

"Water never looked so good to me," said Farrell.

"Me, neither," said Kloor.

"Well, what are we waiting for?" cried Hinton.

They all knelt down on the damp bank of the creek, cupped their hands, and dipped them into the clear, cold stream. For several minutes they drank their fill.

"I feel whole again," said Farrell, sitting back on the bank. "I think I could walk all day to find where this creek leads."

"Hopefully it will lead us to a river and people," said Kloor.

"God willing, it will," said Hinton, rising to his feet and stretching his limbs.

As they resumed their march, Kloor could see that Farrell, despite his hearty words, was soon breathing heavily again and lagging behind. Kloor tried not to get too far ahead of the older man, but he was anxious to keep moving. Their survival depended on finding shelter.

By mid-morning Farrell came to a dead stop. "I can't walk another step in these flying shoes," he said. "They're worn out." He yanked them off his feet, pulled his dress shoes from his overnight bag, and put them on. Farrell left his bag dangling on a tree branch.

"You're not going to leave it there, are you?" asked Hinton.

"Why not?" replied Farrell. "There's nothing in it now that I need. And it was weighing me down."

They hiked onward through the afternoon. Then darkness again descended over the forest. "We'll camp here beside the creek," said Kloor. Hinton estimated they had covered a good eight miles that day. They built another fire but decided not to eat the other pigeons yet. Then they lay down around the crackling fire, hungry, shivering from the cold, and ill-prepared to face another sleepless night.

The fourth day of their ordeal dawned bright and seemed to bring new hope to the three men. Although they had no clear idea where they were, they held on to the belief that the creek would lead them to a town. Civilization and its comforts might lie just around the bend or past the next stand of trees. Following Farrell's example, Kloor and Hinton left their worn-out flying shoes by the campfire and put on their sturdier dress shoes.

Then they began to walk. By late morning, Farrell was exhausted and they stopped for a rest. Hinton built a fire. They cooked and ate the second pigeon, and chewed on some caribou moss they pulled up from the ground. It wasn't very nourishing, but along with the pigeon it took away their hunger pangs for a while.

When the sun was directly overhead, they

resumed their trek. They hadn't gotten very far when Farrell collapsed. Kloor and Hinton rushed to help him, but Farrell pushed Hinton away.

"It's no use," Farrell said hoarsely. "I can't go on."

"Don't be silly," said Hinton. "Of course you can."

"No," replied Farrell abruptly. "You should go on without me."

"That's nonsense," said Kloor. "We couldn't leave you behind."

But Farrell refused to listen. He dug into his pants pocket, pulled out a dirty wad of bills, and thrust it at Hinton.

"What's this?" asked Hinton.

"It's ninety-four dollars," said Farrell. "It's all the money I brought with me. You keep it. If anyone gets through, you will."

Hinton took the cash, not wanting to upset Farrell any further. But together with Kloor, he reached out to lift the older man to his feet.

"Come on, Steve," said Hinton. "You can do it."

"No, I can't," Farrell mumbled feebly. "I'm finished. Leave me here. Save yourselves."

But the other two men ignored his protests.

They propped him up on both sides. Farrell was too weak to resist, and for a while they lumbered along, until Farrell was able to walk on his own again. And so they continued their grim march beside the creek.

Again Farrell began to slow down and drag behind. Hinton and Kloor turned to each other and spoke in hushed voices so Farrell couldn't hear them.

"He may be right, you know," said Hinton. "He may not be able to go on much longer."

"What will we do?" asked Kloor. "We can't just leave him behind."

"We could if we found a safe place for him to wait for us. Then when we find help, we can come back for him."

Kloor shook his head. "How long do you think he would last out here alone? What if a wild animal attacked him?"

"He's got his penknife," said Hinton.

"Big help," Kloor scoffed. "He couldn't defend himself much with that little knife. If he died out here from an animal attack or exposure, we'd never forgive ourselves."

"You're right," said Hinton after a moment's thought. "We'll have to either make it out of here alive together or—"

"Die together," finished Kloor.

Farrell came up behind them. "What are you two chattering on about?" he asked.

"Nothing really," said Hinton. "Steve, why don't you take off that flying suit. It's weighing you down, isn't it?"

Farrell admitted it was and took off the bulky suit, leaving him in his long-john underwear. It was a risky trade-off. While he could move more freely, he was more exposed to the bitter cold. Hinton thought he had the answer. He picked up the flying suit from the frozen ground and carefully wrapped it around Farrell.

"That should keep you warm enough for a while," Hinton said. He wished that he hadn't lost his own flying suit. He supposed it didn't make much difference. None of them were dressed appropriately for the frigid temperatures and they shivered and shook every time they stopped to rest.

This forced them to build a fire at every rest stop, using up more of their precious matches. Hinton looked in the matchbox. There were only four left.

Without the bulky suit restricting his arms and legs, Farrell was able to walk more quickly, but he still struggled to keep up. By the time they stopped for the night, despair had begun to settle in.

As they sat around the campfire, eating the last pigeon, Farrell wondered aloud if he'd ever see his wife and two children again. "It's funny, isn't it?" he said, staring into the bright flames of the fire. "Here I was so worried about my poor daughter sick with scarlet fever. But at least she's warm and safe in bed, with doctors to attend her. Chances are, I'll die out here and she'll, God willing, recover."

Kloor shivered. "Let's not talk about dying," he said.

Hinton disagreed. "We can't ignore the fact that we may not make it out of here alive. We should at least prepare ourselves for the worst."

"What are you talking about?" asked Farrell.

"We should each write farewell letters to our loved ones," Hinton replied. "We can stuff them in our pockets. Then, if we don't make it, when they find our bodies they can send the letters on to our families. It could provide some comfort to them to know we were thinking about them at the end, if it comes to that."

"That's a grim thought," said Kloor.

"I think it's a good idea," said Farrell. "I'd want my wife and children to know what happened if we . . . well, you know."

They all knew. But while Farrell and Hinton wrote their letters by the firelight, Kloor stared into the fire. He didn't want to think about dying. He was the youngest and had too much to live for—a fiancée back home and a long career ahead of him. *Tomorrow,* he told himself as he lay down to try to sleep. *Tomorrow we'll find people. Tomorrow we'll be rescued. Tomorrow the nightmare will end.*

Chapter Six

END OF THE TRAIL

Kloor awoke on the fifth day of their ordeal with a feeling of dread. Despite all their efforts, they were no closer to safety. There was no house, no dog, no people. And now, having eaten the last pigeon, no food. Nothing except a white wilderness that was all but swallowing them up in its vastness. He was beginning to doubt that they would ever get out of this place alive.

Overnight the temperatures had dropped even lower, and the creek had frozen over. While it was a bit slippery, walking on the smooth, ice-covered creek proved to be easier than walking among the trees.

Then, just after midday, their hopes were finally rewarded. The creek widened into a rushing river! Finding a settlement along the river was their best and last hope.

Afraid they might fall through the ice covering the river, the men scrambled back up the riverbank. In his excitement, Farrell lost his footing and crashed to the frozen ground. He realized he couldn't feel his hands any longer. Had frostbite set in? The thought brought a rush of terror to his heart. He quickened his pace and stumbled again, down into a three-foot-deep hole. Farrell cried out, but before his two companions could reach him, he managed to struggle out of the hole himself. Sharp pain ran down his legs. He looked down and saw he had badly scraped his shins. With relief that he could feel his legs and feet at all, Farrell forced himself to get up with a desperate determination. The three men resumed walking, this time following the river.

A short time later, Kloor, moving as quickly as he could and scanning the horizon for signs of civilization, walked right into a thick tree branch that stretched out before him. He went down to the ground, stunned by the blow. The branch had also caught on his flight suit and torn a large hole in the side of it. He looked into the hole but saw no sign of blood. As he rose to his feet, he cursed to himself for not looking where he was going.

Hinton was the next to go down. He tried his best to keep up with Kloor, but his foot caught on a gnarled root and he fell headlong to the hardened earth. Kloor heard his anguished cry and turned. Hinton waved a hand to indicate he was all right and rose heavily to his feet. Kloor gave him a thumbs-up but in his mind he began to wonder how long the two other men could last. He considered for the first time the awful possibility that he might soon be on his own, alone in the wilderness.

Then Kloor saw something that made his spirits soar again. Two deep parallel lines in the snow. "Look!" Kloor shouted back to the other two. "Tracks!"

Hinton and Farrell rushed to catch up to Kloor, moving as fast as their bodies could take them.

When they reached him, they gave a feeble cheer. There in front of them were sled tracks! There was no mistake. This was their first sign of humans!

"Come on!" Kloor cried, voice cracking and legs pumping in the deep snow. Doggedly, they followed the tracks along the river.

An hour passed, then two. Exhausted as they were, the men moved faster than they had ever moved before. A desperate but genuine hope drove them on.

Soon the river emptied into a huge lake. At its edge, the tracks simply disappeared.

Their eyes searched the ice desperately for a sign of the sled tracks.

"Gone!" cried Farrell. "The tracks have just vanished into thin air."

"It's not possible," said Kloor, shaking his head vigorously. "The sled must have gone onto the lake. It might not leave any tracks on the ice."

"If that's so, then we can find the tracks again on the other side," reasoned Hinton, the excitement rising in his voice.

"Well," cried Farrell, suddenly energized, "what

are we waiting for? Let's go!"

They tested the lake ice by tapping their feet on it to see if it was strong enough to hold their weight. Convinced they were safe to continue, they began crossing. Kloor again quickly took the lead. He could feel his heart pounding in his chest with every slippery step.

They were more than halfway across when Kloor saw it. The figure of a man on the far side of the lake.

Kloor couldn't make out his features, only that he was standing still and appeared to be staring directly at Kloor. He was sure of it. "Hello! Hello!" he cried as loud as he could, waving his arms wildly in the air. The man didn't move. He just continued to stare. Then, without warning, the man turned and started running away.

"No! No!" cried Kloor. "Help! Come back! Come back!"

But his cries only seemed to make the man flee all the faster. Kloor fell to his knees on the ice and covered his face with his hands. Here was their first and last hope and he was leaving them. Leaving them stranded in the wilderness, leaving them to die.

We have finally reached it, Kloor thought, *the end of the trail.*

Chapter Seven

AN UNEXPECTED MEETING

Kloor slowly got to his feet, his eyes still focused on the running figure in front of him. Hinton and Farrell ran up to him, panting heavily.

"We've got to catch up to that man," said Hinton breathlessly. "He's our last hope."

Kloor nodded. Of course he was right. It couldn't end this way. Not when they had come this far.

They began to run toward the figure in the distance. Then, suddenly, Farrell slowed. "Look!" he cried. "He's stopping!"

The man had stopped running and was looking directly at them.

"Let's go," yelled Kloor, "before he decides to take flight again."

Within moments they reached the stranger's side. He was a large, middle-aged man with brown skin and long, dark hair. Kloor guessed he was Native American. Farrell and Hinton jabbered away, asking questions, yet the man simply shook his head.

"I don't think he speaks English. If we can't communicate with words, perhaps this will work," said Kloor. He took out a crumpled cigarette from his pocket and offered it to the man, who smiled and took it.

"We seem to be getting somewhere," said Farrell. "Do we have anything else we can give him?" he asked Hinton. "To show him our gratitude."

Hinton reached into his pocket and pulled out a dollar bill. The man took it and examined it carefully. This gave Hinton another idea.

"Are we in the United States?" he asked, pointing to the bill.

The man shook his head. "Canada," he replied.

"He does know some English!" Farrell cried.

"So we're in Canada," mused Kloor. "We really did get off course."

The man they had met was Native Canadian not Native American. It quickly became apparent the men's words would get them nowhere, so they communicated as best they could with hand gestures. They motioned to their mouths with their hands. They were hungry. The man nodded and pointed into the distance.

"He must be telling us his house is nearby," said Farrell, excitement rising in his voice. The man motioned for them to follow him and started to run.

"Come on!" cried Kloor. "We can't lose him now."

"Not when we can get somewhere dry and warm and out of this blasted cold at last."

The men did their best to keep up, but quickly lagged behind. In a short time, a sled pulled by two horses appeared in the distance. The driver, also native, stopped and spoke to the other man. Their rescuer pointed to the three of them as he spoke in his own language.

"Look! He's coming for us!" cried Hinton.

When the sled stopped in front of them Hinton smiled and thanked the driver for giving them a lift. The man nodded, his expression neutral.

"I wonder if this is the sled that made the tracks we followed," whispered Farrell.

"It could be," said Hinton. "Either way, I'm grateful we found it—or he found us."

The other two nodded in agreement and climbed aboard. Farrell needed Hinton and Kloor to help him up into the sled. Kloor was worried that the frostbite on Farrell's hands was serious enough that he might lose them. But that would have to wait. The three of them flopped down in the sled, and it took off swiftly across the snow.

In just a few minutes the driver brought the horses to a halt in front of a weathered shack.

"Well, it may not be exactly home, sweet home, but it'll do," said Farrell.

Each man climbed off the sled and thanked the driver, who nodded. He said a few words in his native language to their rescuer, who had followed behind them, and drove off. The inside of the shack was small, but it was warm. Their host revived glowing embers in the makeshift fireplace and added more wood to the flames. He

gestured for the men to sit on a wooden bench before the blaze, but Kloor saw that Farrell was barely able to stand.

Hinton turned to their host. He gestured to Farrell, who had plopped down on the bench, his eyes closed. "Our friend," he said slowly. "He needs to rest. Is there a place he can lie down?"

The man looked at Farrell and seemed to understand. He gestured to a bunk a few feet away from where they stood in the tiny hut. Hinton and Kloor thanked him and got Farrell to the bunk. Within moments, he was asleep and snoring loudly.

The man smiled and the two others laughed. "Asleep like a baby," said Hinton.

"I never heard a baby snore like that," quipped Kloor.

The man gestured back to the bench and the two men sat and warmed themselves by the fire. Then their host went to a corner of the hut that served as his kitchen. He filled a kettle with water and put it on the fire, brewing tea. He gave the grateful men mugs filled with the steaming beverage. Next he brought them boiled fish in wooden bowls.

Kloor took a bite or two and stopped. "I can't eat anymore," he said to Hinton. "It's delicious, but my stomach must have shrunk from the little we've eaten these past days."

"Me too," agreed Hinton, after taking a few bites.

The men were afraid they would offend their host by not eating, but fortunately, he was preoccupied with stoking the fire and didn't seem to notice how little they ate.

In a short time, the men heard voices outside the hut. Another native man, much younger than their host, entered. His long, loose hair was jet black and his brown eyes glistened.

"My name is Erland Vincent," he said. "The man who brought you in his sled told me you were here."

"You speak English!" exclaimed Hinton.

"Yes," said Vincent. "I am a member of the Cree Nation, like Tom Marks, the man who rescued you. We will bring you to the trading post at Moose

Factory. They will take good care of you there."

"Moose Factory?" repeated Hinton.

"That's the village where the Hudson's Bay Company trading post is located," explained Vincent. "It's where many Cree, like Tom, bring their furs to sell. It's not far. Just a mile from here."

"Well, what are we waiting for?" said Kloor.

Marks went to the bunk and gently awakened Farrell, who seemed better after his short nap. Kloor and Hinton told him where they were going and the three men said their warm goodbyes to their host.

"We can never repay you for your kindness," said Kloor. Then he pressed a handful of dollars and all the remaining cigarettes he had into Tom Marks's hands.

"Thank you," Marks said.

"We wouldn't be alive if not for you," said Hinton, embracing Marks in an awkward hug.

Farrell, clearly overcome with emotion, blurted out "Darn right" to Hinton's statement and patted Marks on the back.

They went outside, where a crowd of Cree were

gathered around, staring at them.

"What are they doing here?" Farrell asked Vincent.

"They came to see you," Vincent explained. "You are already big news in Moose Factory."

The men laughed and climbed back into the same sled that had brought them to Marks's hut. The sled took off and they sat back, eagerly awaiting the next chapter in their adventure.

THE CREE PEOPLE

The Cree people were hunting moose and caribou and trapping beaver in the forests of North America long before the arrival of Europeans. They lived in birch-bark wigwams and paddled canoes on waterways rich with fish. When the Europeans came, the Cree traded their animal pelts for other goods.

The Canadian Cree mostly live in the region from Alberta to Québec, as well as portions of the Plains region in Saskatchewan. The American Cree live in the Rocky Mountains region and along parts of the Atlantic Coast. Few Cree today speak their traditional language. Most speak French in Canada and English in the United States. While some Cree continue to make their livelihood from trapping, others work in the mining industry or frozen fish factories.

See more about the Cree people at the end of this book.

Chapter Eight

THE TRADING POST

The sled flew across the snowy countryside. The icy wind felt cold but refreshing on the men's faces. The landscape quickly changed from the natural world to one made by humans. They passed buildings and homes. Farrell thought he could smell smoke from home fires and the sweet scent of meat cooking. The sled finally came to a halt in front of a large wooden structure.

"This is the Hudson's Bay Company trading post," said Vincent. "As you can see, they're waiting for you." Some thirty-five men, including several native Cree, were standing outside the trading post, shouting merrily and waving their arms in greeting.

As the three men climbed out of the sled, a tall, imposing man with a grizzled beard stepped forward to shake their hands.

"I'm William Rackham," he said. "I'm the agent here for Hudson's Bay Company. We're happy to have you as our guests and we want to hear the whole story of how you got here."

"That will take some time to tell," said Hinton.

"Time is something we have plenty of here," said Rackham. "But first let's get you inside, where it's warm."

The trading post's main building was spacious and inviting, with a large stone fireplace and wood furniture. The three men sat around the blazing fire in comfortable, cushioned chairs as the men of the trading post listened intently to their story. When they got to the part about the balloon crashing in the trees, Rackham called Vincent and whispered something to him. Then the young Cree left with several others.

"What did you say to him?" Kloor asked.

"I asked Erland if he would go out and look

for your balloon," Rackham said. "He was very happy to do so."

"Thank you," said Kloor. "I'm sure the US Navy would appreciate it if they found it."

After the men had finished their story, they were allowed to rest in beds with real mattresses while a dinner was prepared for them. One of the postmen who had medical experience treated Farrell's frostbitten hands and feet. To his great relief, Farrell was told that the frostbite had been caught and treated in time and he wouldn't lose any fingers or toes. But his full recovery would take months.

The dinner prepared for them was roasted moose meat and potatoes. By then, their stomachs had digested the fish stew and they were ready for more. All three declared it was the best meal they ever ate.

"Better than pigeon?" joked Rackham.

"The poor pigeons!" sighed Hinton. "They made the ultimate sacrifice, and we're grateful for it."

"We are truly grateful to you for helping us,"

Kloor told Rackham.

"And we're just as grateful to have your company," said Rackham. "It isn't often we get visitors. It's lonely up here in northern Ontario."

"We can imagine," said Hinton. "What with these terrible winters."

Rackham smiled. "What are you talking about?" he said. "This is the mildest winter we've had in Moose Factory in twenty years!"

Everyone in the room laughed, and the three balloonists realized now, more than ever, how lucky they really were.

A day later, as the balloonists and the trading post men sat around the fire talking, the big wooden door opened and Erland Vincent came in with his team of Cree.

"Sorry, we did not find your balloon," said Vincent.

"It was near a house," said Kloor. "If that's helpful."

Vincent laughed. "There is no house in that area," he said. "What you saw, I'm afraid, was probably a haystack."

Kloor gulped. The hope of finding the house had kept the men alive. And now it had never existed at all.

Vincent continued, "But the barking dog you heard was there—a husky actually. It was caught in a beaver trap. We let it go and it came back with us."

"Well then," said Farrell, with good cheer. "Your search party wasn't a complete waste of time."

During the next several days, as Farrell slowly recuperated, Kloor and Hinton enjoyed the simple pleasures of the trading post. They played cards and dominoes with the men at the post, read books, and collaborated on a written account of their ordeal. When Farrell was better, they shared the written account with him.

The next day, the men celebrated Christmas with the Cree and the trading post workers. Each man was given a gift from the trading post Christmas tree. Farrell got a bag full of candy that he vowed not to eat, but would bring back to his sick daughter Emily. Rackham dressed up as Santa Claus in his fur-trimmed over-coat and sealskin boots. Kloor, Hinton, and Farrell combed out strands of rope to make a bigger set of whiskers for him to wear over his beard.

One afternoon before they departed from the post, Kloor wrote a letter to his father. He apologized for causing him worry and pain about his disappearance, but added, "If you can realize how near we were to death and how miraculously we were snatched from death, you would forgive all."

But, as the men were about to find out, their ordeal was not over yet. When they were strong enough, they would have to travel another 180 miles south through the wilderness on dogsleds to reach the tiny town of Mattice, where the nearest railroad station was located.

This final leg of their journey would prove as challenging as anything they had already experienced.

THE HUDSON'S BAY COMPANY

The Hudson's Bay Company, founded in 1670, is the oldest continuously operating commercial venture in North America. Two young French traders in Canada, then the French colony of New France, came up with the idea of a business dealing in animal pelts. When the governor of New France turned down their proposal, the traders took their idea to the English, who were interested. In 1677, Prince Rupert, the cousin of King Charles II of England, took control of the project and granted the company a charter (a written contract to do business).

The Hudson's Bay Company established itself in the vast region surrounding the body of water it was named for. The company built trading posts and forts throughout the region where anyone—native people and Europeans—could come to trade their animal pelts for guns, knives, and other manufactured goods. The pelts were then shipped to England, where they were used to adorn expensive hats and clothing.

Competition from other fur traders led the company to expand across Canada. By the 1800s, the demand for furs lessened and the company turned its attention to a thriving wholesale business, featuring liquor, canned salmon, coffee, tea, and tobacco.

Chapter Nine

THE LAST LEG

Kloor, Farrell, and Hinton left Moose Factory for Mattice on December 28, fourteen days after crashing into the wilderness. But this time they would not be traveling alone. A team of Cree men accompanied them with two sleds, each pulled by four husky dogs. Farrell, whose feet had not fully recovered from frostbite, rode in one of the sleds. Kloor and Hinton, who had been practicing snowshoeing for eleven days at the trading post, were ready to try out their new skill. The men had insulated clothing, a good supply of moose meat for food, and sturdy tents to keep them warm at night.

But despite these supplies, it was a grueling trek. All their practice did not make Kloor and Hinton any more adept at snowshoeing than when they started. They felt clumsy and uncoordinated, and within a short time, they were completely exhausted. The snowshoes felt like heavy weights on their feet. Each step became a mighty effort. Hinton suffered from a stinging attack on the nerves in his legs called *mal de racquet* by the French Canadians. He managed to tie a piece of rope to the back of each snowshoe and lift it at each step with his hands to help relieve the pain. But there was no relief for their aching legs when, at the end of each day's journey, they had to climb the steep bank of the river they followed to make camp for the night.

After a few days, they ran into their first blizzard. Fat flakes fell like confetti from a white sky, driven into their faces by blasting wind. Visibility fell to near zero and they couldn't see their hands in front of their faces, let alone the trail ahead. At times Hinton and Kloor would cry out to one another or to Farrell on the sled

and follow the answering voices to find their way back to the others.

A couple of times, one of them wandered blindly away from the main party and would have been lost in the blizzard if not for one of their Cree companions, who found the lost man, took him by the hand, and brought him back to the trail. One morning the snow was falling so thickly that they had to give up after just one hour and set up camp again. They had no sooner struggled through one blizzard when they ran headlong into a second . . . and then a third, all within the first week.

But the snow wasn't all they had to deal with. Temperatures reached as low as −30 degrees Fahrenheit. The men kept nearly every inch of their bodies covered with clothing, gloves, and hats to prevent frostbite. But their noses remained exposed and became frostbitten. It got so cold at times that moisture from their breath froze to their eyelids. The thongs that bound Kloor's and Hinton's snowshoes to their ankles froze and shortened, causing their feet to cramp and blister.

As terrible as the blizzard conditions were, the men could be grateful for one thing. They hadn't had to face the driving snow when they were on their own after the balloon crash. If they had wandered into a blizzard, they probably never would have found the sled tracks. Never run into Tom Marks. Never made it to the trading post. They would have died alone in the wilderness.

Their current path was mostly unbroken and covered in frozen snow. Kloor and Hinton had to take their turns going ahead of the dogs to tramp it down at best they could. In some spots the trail was thick with slush and it caked on their snow-shoes, making them heavier than ever. At times the two men had to stop and clean off the slush with hands trembling from the freezing cold.

"This is hopeless," muttered Hinton to Kloor, struggling to be heard above the shrieking wind. "We can't go on like this."

"I know," said Kloor. "We'll never make it this way."

One of the Cree, running alongside them, saw their predicament and knew they had had enough.

He motioned to the second sled, behind the one that Farrell rode in. "Get in," he said. "Let the dogs do the work."

Kloor feared their weight would be too much for the dogs to pull, but the Cree insisted. So the two men hopped onto the sled and removed the snowshoes from their feet.

"Thank God," said Hinton. "I couldn't have gone another fifty yards with those things on my feet. It's torture."

"Yes," agreed Kloor. "Now we can sit back and enjoy the ride."

But their enjoyment didn't last long. The sled began to slow down and the dogs seemed to be struggling. "I knew we were too much weight for the sled," said Kloor.

"No," said the Cree who ran alongside the sled. "It's not you. The ice is freezing on the sled's runners. That's what's slowing us down." He called to two of his companions and the three of them got behind the sled and pushed to help the dogs. Three other Cree did the same on the other sled, which carried Farrell.

Kloor and Hinton were grateful to the Cree for their experience, fortitude, and goodwill in such difficult conditions. But by the end of the next day, it was clear that the strain of the journey was taking its toll on everyone. The Cree men were huffing and puffing and slowing their pace in the face of the unrelenting snow and cold. During a rest stop, Kloor and Hinton saw the Cree leader say something to one of his companions. Then this man and a second man started running back down the trail toward Moose Factory.

Hinton exchanged tense looks with Kloor. What was happening? Were their guides giving up and abandoning them in the wilderness? Hinton felt he had to know the truth one way or the other.

"Why are they going back?" he asked the Cree leader.

The Cree's face broke into a wide, reassuring grin. "To get fresh dogs," he replied. "We'll never make it to Mattice with these poor huskies. They need a rest. Just like we do." Kloor and Hinton breathed a collective sigh of relief. Without these resourceful men, they would have no hope of ever making it to Mattice.

DOGSLEDDING

Dogsleds had been a main means of transportation and communication in the Far North for a thousand years before Kloor and his companions used them to travel to Mattice. Native peoples like the Inuit were the first to use dogs to pull sleds across the frozen wasteland. The Russian explorers and traders who came to Alaska in the 1700s paired the dogs side by side and added a lead dog who would carry out the human sled driver's commands. Since then, dogsleds have been the main means of carrying everything from firewood to mail in remote places where there are no roads. Alaskan huskies are the primary breed trained as sled dogs, and their strength, determination, and courage is legendary. Probably the most famous sled dog is Balto. In 1925, serum from Seattle, Washington, was desperately needed to end a diphtheria outbreak in Nome, Alaska. Twenty teams of sled dogs carried the medicine 674 miles (1,085 km) over six days to Nome. Balto led the dogs in the last leg of the difficult trek. A statue of Balto stands on a rock in New York's Central Park. In 1995 an animated movie about the thrilling rescue, *Balto*, was released.

On a frigid January day, Kloor noted his twenty-third birthday. When they made camp for the night, despite the bitter conditions, the Cree managed to bake a small cake out of flour and eggs. Hinton found a nub of a wax candle, stuck it in the cake, and lit the candle with his last match. They all sang "Happy Birthday" in a ragged chorus and drank cups of hot tea. Tears fell from Kloor's eyes.

"A birthday's nothing to be sad about, Kid," said Farrell.

"I was just thinking how close I've come in the last few weeks to not making it to twenty-three," Kloor said, his voice growing hoarse.

Hinton patted him on the shoulder. "Make a

wish and blow out the candle," he said.

Kloor did. No one asked what he wished for. They all knew it could be only one thing—to reach Mattice alive. Then they all devoured the cake.

Farrell, still hungry, eyed the candy in his Christmas bag.

"Go ahead and eat one," said Hinton.

"No," said Farrell. "They're for Sis. I won't touch them." He fingered the tiny British flag, another memento in the bag for his sick daughter, and then closed it. He had made his own wish that night—that Sis would have fully recovered from the scarlet fever.

Kloor's wish, at least, came true. On January 11, 1921, after fifteen days on the trail, the small party straggled into Mattice.

Although the three lost balloonists didn't know it, their disappearance had caused a major stir back in the States. The fact that Hinton was a celebrated pilot from his transatlantic flight a few years earlier drew the nation's attention. Newspapers around the nation took notice of the missing balloon. The Rockaway Air Station had received word that the men and balloon had been seen flying over Wells, New York, on the evening of December 13. Naval officials at the station held out hope that the balloon had come down in an isolated region and that the men were alive. Their worst fears were that the balloon had been caught in a tree and that the men were unable to get down from it. The navy sent messages to its ships and naval stations to be on the lookout for the missing men. Army planes flew daily out of Albany searching for them in the Adirondacks.

Now word of their miraculous rescue in Canada had reached Mattice. The tiny community was overflowing with reporters, photographers, and newsreel cameramen from the United States and Canada. They were all eager to see the three men and interview them about their adventure.

The navy had issued an order that the three men were to share no details about their experience publicly until they had handed in an official report. This didn't deter the reporters, though, who swarmed each member of the party as he came in.

Kloor arrived in town first, at about two fifteen

p.m. His first words to the reporters who met him were "I feel fine. We're all right. All I ask is that I get to a fire." He was soon followed by Hinton. Farrell, well behind them, didn't get in for another half hour. And that was what quickly led to trouble.

Chapter Ten

A FALLING-OUT

Navy officials hustled Kloor and Hinton into a private railcar belonging to the superintendent of the Canadian National Railway. Here they could be interviewed about their experiences before talking to the press. Farrell, however, was waylaid by reporters who whisked him into the cabin of the local Hudson's Bay Company's clerk with the promise of hot tea and a meal. They told Farrell that they already knew about some of their ordeal from letters Hinton had written to his wife from Moose Factory. They had been published in the newspaper the *New York World*.

Farrell couldn't believe what he was hearing.

It had been Hinton who suggested they work together on their story. But he had gone back on his promise and shared details of their adventure with his wife and the media. Even worse, the reporters informed him that in his letters, Hinton had portrayed Farrell in a bad light. He shared details about Farrell's inability to go on and his wanting the other two to leave him behind. Upset, exhausted, and confused, Farrell began to tell his version of their ordeal to the reporters. He was almost finished when Hinton entered the cabin. Hinton looked around at the eager faces of the reporters and at Farrell and knew at once what was happening.

"Come on, Steve," he said. "You need to come with me. The navy has a nice lunch waiting for us in a railcar. Let's go."

Farrell didn't move. He simply glared at Hinton, his eyes on fire.

"Get out, you rat!" Farrell cried.

Hinton ignored his outburst. He drew closer to Farrell and spoke in a low voice. "These men are taking down every word you say and it will all be printed," he said.

"Get away from me, you double-crosser!" said Farrell. "I know why you don't want me to speak to them."

Hinton put a hand on Farrell's shoulder and Farrell pushed it away. Then Farrell pulled back one arm and shot his fist out, hitting Hinton on the jaw. The reporters gasped as Hinton fell to the floor. He lay there for a few seconds, in a daze. Several reporters grabbed Farrell to prevent him from attacking Hinton again. Others urged Hinton to leave to avoid further trouble. Hinton got to his feet, looked at his old friend, and left without uttering another word.

Kloor could see something was very wrong as soon as Hinton returned to the railroad car.

"It's finished," said Hinton.

"What?" asked Kloor, speaking in a whisper so the navy officials present wouldn't hear.

"Steve's spilled the beans," replied Hinton. "He's told the reporters all about what happened. Good luck trying to sell our written account now."

One of the naval officers stepped up to them.

"Where is Lieutenant Farrell?" he asked. "We don't want to start lunch without him."

Hinton was about to make an excuse for Farrell's absence when the door opened and Farrell walked in. He apologized for keeping them waiting and shook hands with Kloor, but refused to even look at Hinton.

The lunch was a tense affair for the three men. Kloor sat between Farrell and Hinton, which kept the peace, but once they left the railcar, the arguing continued.

"He betrayed us," said Farrell to Kloor. "You should be as angry at him as I am."

"Maybe I did say too much to my wife," admitted Hinton. "But I definitely told her not to say anything to the newspapers. She did that on her own."

Farrell wasn't satisfied. "Then what about those things you said about me—that I didn't want to go on, that I gave up. That I wanted you to leave me behind."

Hinton and Kloor exchanged knowing looks. They both knew the truth, a truth that Farrell would prefer not to remember. But Hinton knew he had to make peace with his colleague, especially with the whole world watching.

"I'm sorry, Steve," he said. "I exaggerated what happened. I didn't mean to make you look bad. And everything I said in that letter I said in confidence."

"And now it's splashed across the front page of the *New York World*," insisted Farrell. "You've ruined my good name! That's what you've done!"

"Look, both of you," said Kloor, playing the mediator, "it's not too late to set things straight. We've got to face those reporters again before we catch the train for Toronto in the morning. Let's patch things up right now by shaking hands."

The two men eyed each other cautiously. Then Hinton reached out a hand and, after a moment's hesitation, Farrell did the same.

The next evening the three men met reporters before catching the train for Toronto. Kloor read a prepared statement, explaining that the quarrel between Hinton and Farrell was "the outcome of overwrought minds brought on by the hardships and grueling struggles that had to be endured on the trip over the trail to Mattice . . . Such petty quarrels as may have occurred will not lessen our affection for one another." For his part, Hinton admitted that he had exaggerated his descriptions of Farrell in his letters to his wife.

When they arrived in Toronto a crowd of six hundred people turned out to greet them. Hinton tried to compensate for what he had said earlier about Farrell with kinder, if not truer, words. "Farrell is the hero . . . He broke the trail and did the hardest work," he declared to the crowd.

"Where are the pigeons?" one man asked. Kloor grinned and rubbed his stomach in reply.

The next morning they arrived by train in New York City in the middle of a rainstorm. Despite the bad weather, a cheering crowd of ten thousand had turned out to greet the heroes. "We're all good shipmates again," Kloor reassured the crowd. "That other little affair was just the devil of the wilds that cuts loose in every man's blood in the North . . ."

A six-mile parade accompanied the three men

to the Rockaway Air Station. Three bands played music and the air was filled with floating miniature gas bags in honor of the balloonists.

While the public hailed the men as heroes, the navy wasn't so sure. It held a court of inquiry to judge if any neglect or misconduct was responsible for the loss of the balloon and the men's subsequent ordeal. The inquiry ended with no charges leveled against any of the three.

"There was no one particular hero, and we do not consider ourselves heroes," Kloor told the court. "Each one did the best that was in him. Sacrifice after sacrifice prevailed."

EPILOGUE

After their amazing adventure faded from the newspaper headlines, Kloor, Hinton, and Farrell went on with their lives. Louis Kloor continued to fly balloons for the navy and years later retired to San Joaquin County, California, with his wife, where he died in 1971.

Stephen Farrell spent seven months after their return to New York in a state of "neurasthenia exhaustion," which required medical care. Today he would probably be diagnosed with post-traumatic stress disorder (PTSD). He retired from the navy in 1926, after thirty years of service. When World War II began, Farrell tried to reenlist, but was rejected due to a heart condition. He spent his last years in Watertown, New York, and died of a heart attack on July 12, 1946. He was sixty-eight years old.

Walter Hinton turned his interest in aviation southward and attempted to make the first successful flight from New York to Rio de Janeiro, Brazil. On his initial try, his plane crashed off the coast of Cuba and he was rescued from shark-infested waters, clinging to the wing of his plane. On his second try, he succeeded. Hinton went on to make the first aerial exploration of Brazil's Amazon River by hydroplane. He founded and was president of the Aviation Institute of USA in 1927 in Washington, DC. There he published periodicals promoting flying, including *Opportunities in Aviation* and *Aviation Progress*. He became an enthusiastic spokesperson for aviation, taking his message across the United States.

Hinton retired to Pompano Beach, Florida. One of the thrills of his later years was being a special guest on a transatlantic flight of the supersonic jet the Concorde. The flight that took him nineteen days back in 1919 now took under four hours!

In July 1981, a few months before his death, Hinton was honored by the Brazilian government for his exploration by plane of the Amazon. Speaking of his achievements in early aviation he had this to say: "There weren't many people interested in it in those days. The majority of them thought it was just a bunch of daredevils. But I'm still very proud of everything." And that sense of pride would have surely included surviving the ordeal in the Canadian wilderness after that fateful balloon crash of December 1920.

THE HISTORY AND TRADITIONS OF THE CREE PEOPLE

PENNY M. THOMAS, Fisher River Cree Nation/ Peguis First Nation, author of *Nimoshom and His Bus* and *Powwow Counting in Cree*

The Cree people of North America, who also identify themselves as the Nehiyawak, make up more than 300,000 of the Canadian and American population today. The majority of Cree people live in Canada in the Subartic region from Alberta to Quebec, as well as Saskatchewan, Manitoba, Ontario, and the Northwest Territories. In the United States, the Cree reside in Montana and North Dakota.

The word Nehiyaw stems from the Cree number four, *Newo*, and means a four-bodied person. The Cree people believe that the self is made up of four different quadrants: the physical, the emotional, the mental, and the spiritual. Along with many other indigenous people, sometimes called First Nations people in Canada, the Cree believe that keeping these four areas in balance is the key to good health.

The Cree people hunted, gathered, fished, and lived in different areas of Canada and the United States long before European settlers came. Depending on where they lived, they hunted game such as, moose, elk, deer, and buffalo. When big game was sparse, they often lived off smaller animals such as rabbit and beaver. The Cree were nomadic; they followed the herds of game animals and visited specific areas where they gathered berries, roots, wild vegetables, and medicinal plants. Fish was also a large part of their diet. Because of their nomadic lifestyle, they lived in tipis and wigwams, which were easy to disassemble and transport.

After the European settlers came, the Cree traded with them for items such as guns, beads, blankets and foodstuffs. Beaver pelt was most commonly what they traded for other goods. Eventually, the Cree replaced their tipis and wigwams with canvas tents and wood cabins. Their traditional clothing, made of animal hides and skins, evolved to incorporate cloth.

In 1876, almost fifty years before Tom Marks met and rescued Kloor, Hinton, and Farrell, the government of Canada, which was made up of European settlers, passed the Indian Act. The Indian Act allowed the government to control most aspects of aboriginal life, including Indian status, land, resources, wills, and education. Part of the act made it mandatory for First Nations children to attend residential schools, or boarding schools. Children as young as four were sent to the schools, where they were forced to learn English and were punished if they spoke their first language. Because of this, the Cree, along with many other tribes in Canada, lost their language and many other cultural practices. In 1996, the last residential school was closed. The Iroquois Seventh Generation Principle says all choices have effects for seven generations. It is believed by many that overcoming the effects of the residential schools will take seven generations.

First Nation people believe in respecting nature and all living things, and that the great creator Kitchi-Manitou (Cree interpretation) gave everything in nature a spirit, even inanimate objects. Connection to the creator is established through ceremony, prayer, fasting, visions, and dreams. Storytelling is key to passing on these traditions, to teaching life lessons and medicinal knowledge, and for healing the mind and body.

AUTHOR'S NOTE

The story of survival you have just read actually happened. The three men who experienced it in the winter of 1920–21 were real people. However, some of the details were made up by me, the author. Why? For one thing, the information about the events depicted is limited. Nearly all that is known about this adventure in the Canadian wilderness is taken from newspaper articles written at the time it happened. None of the three men, to my knowledge, wrote a published account of the events. To fill in the gaps, I had to add details. For example, Kloor's birthday did take place during their trek to Mattice, but I created the details of that celebration. Secondly, I wanted to have the men think and speak for themselves as they lived this gripping story. That meant imagining their thoughts from their personal point of view and giving them words to speak. Where I could find their actual recorded words in newspaper accounts, I used them, but most of the dialogue had to be invented. Finally, I added specific details and descriptions to make the story more exciting and real for the reader, such as each man's falling down in their desperate journey along the river.

Having said this, many of the most dramatic moments of the story were already there—Hinton misplacing his flight suit as he searches for water, Farrell telling the other two to leave him behind, their rescue by Tom Marks, and the fight between Hinton and Farrell witnessed by the reporters in Mattice. It proves once again, that fact is often stranger, and more fascinating, than fiction.

SELECTED BIBLIOGRAPHY

"Aeronauts Rest on Eve of Inquiry." *The New York Times*. Jan. 16, 1921. New York, New York.

"Balloon Drops Navy Airmen in Canadian Wilderness." *Popular Mechanics*. Chicago, IL: March 1921.

"Balloon Flight Will Be Probed." *The Daily Telegraph*. Jan. 13, 1921. Bluefield, West Virginia.

"Balloonists Back on American Soil." *The New York Times*. Jan. 14, 1921. New York, New York.

"Balloonists Welcomed by Rockaway Citizens." *The Flathead Courier*. Jan. 17, 1921. Polson, Montana.

"Battle for Life in Frozen Northland First Told by One of Lost Balloonists." *The Philadelphia Inquirer*. Jan. 9, 1921. Philadelphia, Pennsylvania.

Dash, Mike. "World War I: 100 Years Later: Closing the Pigeon Gap." Smithsonian.com.

"Fatted Pig Killed for Feast for Kloor." *The Boston Globe*. Jan. 12, 1921. Boston, Massachusetts.

"Kloor Praises Companions in Balloon Flight." *Cornell Daily Sun*. Jan. 19, 1921. Ithaca, New York.

"Lt. Kloor Tells of Balloon Failure." *The New York Times*. Jan. 19, 1921. New York, New York.

Martin, Bob. "Ordeal: Lost and Facing Death in a Remote Frozen Forest." Smashwords, 2013.

"Naval Airman Tells of Trip." *The Richford Journal and Gazette*. Jan. 21, 1921. Richford, Vermont.

"Navy Balloonists All Friendly, On Way to New York." *The St. Louis Post-Dispatch*. Jan. 13, 1921. St. Louis, Missouri.

"Stephen Farrell on Lost Balloon." *The New York Times*. July 13, 1946. New York, New York.

"Story of Flight Told by Farrell." *The New York Times*. Jan. 12, 1921. New York, New York.

"Walter Hinton, 92; Aviation Pioneer." *The New York Times*. Oct. 31, 1981. New York, New York.

"Watch Trail Airmen Take." *Buffalo Evening News*. Jan. 6, 1921. Buffalo, New York.

ABOUT THE AUTHOR

STEVEN OTFINOSKI has written more than two hundred books for children and young adults, including the Step into History series for Scholastic and nine titles in the Tangled History series for Capstone Press. Three of his YA books have been named Books for the Teen Age by the New York Public Library. He has an MFA in creative writing from Fairfield University in Connecticut, where he teaches composition and creative writing. Steve is also an award-winning playwright with more than sixty productions of his plays to his credit. His children's theater company, History Alive!, presents one-person shows about people from American history to schoolchildren. He, his wife, Beverly, and Jake, their mini Aussie shepherd, divide their time between Connecticut and the Berkshires in Massachusetts, where he reviews summer theater for the *New England Theatre Journal.*

ABOUT THE EDITOR

MICHAEL TEITELBAUM has been a writer and editor of children's books for more than twenty-five years. He worked on staff as an editor at Golden Books, Grossett & Dunlop, and Macmillan. As a writer, Michael's fiction work includes *The Scary States of America*, fifty short stories—one from each state—all about the paranormal, published by Random House, and *The Very Hungry Zombie: A Parody,* done with artist extraordinaire Jon Apple, published by Skyhorse. His nonfiction work includes *Jackie Robinson: Champion for Equality*, published by Sterling; *The Baseball Hall of Fame*, a two-volume encyclopedia, published by Grolier; *Sports in America, 1980–89*, published by Chelsea House; and *Great Moments in Women's Sports* and *Great Inventions: Radio and Television*, both published by World Almanac Library. Michael lives with his wife, Sheleigh, and two talkative cats in the beautiful Catskill Mountains of upstate New York.

Turn the page for a sneak peek at the next
DEATH-DEFYING GREAT ESCAPE!

Chapter One

UNDER SIEGE

Preston, England—13th of November, 1715

William Maxwell, 5th Earl and Lord of Nithsdale, clutched his musket with sweaty hands and gazed at the battle before him. All around, Scottish rebels were being ripped apart by British artillery, their blood spilling on the cobblestone street.

The tall, bearded Maxwell, or Lord Nithsdale as he was better known, crouched behind a wooden barrel as musket and cannonballs flew through the sky overhead. Black smoke from burning houses clogged the air and reddened every man's eyes, making it difficult to see.

The kilted Scottish Highlanders—Nithsdale's comrades from the mountains—were fighting to keep a hold over Preston, the northern British town they had invaded just four days earlier. Unfortunately, they were greatly outnumbered by red-coated British soldiers. They'd set up barricades to keep the British from entering the city, but holding them became increasingly difficult as the redcoats swarmed the town like fire ants.

Cold sweat ran down Nithsdale's bearded face, and his thumping heart felt as if it was going to beat out of his chest. He peeked around the wooden barrel and saw another Scotsman fall, killed by British musket fire as they tried to hold the makeshift barricade.

What are you doing? Nithsdale scolded himself silently. *You're the commanding officer in charge of that barricade! Get up and fight!*

And yet he stayed hunkered down. He thought of his wife, Winifred, and his son, both safe back home in Scotland, and wanted nothing more than to be back with them at their castle.

Why did I ever agree to go to battle? I'm no soldier!

Something zoomed through the air close by. Nithsdale jerked back as a cannonball crashed down on the street a few feet away, showering him with piercing shards of cobblestone fragments. The heavy iron ball bounced and then tore through a crowd of oncoming Scots like they were nothing more than sheets of paper.

The men's screams almost drowned out the gunfire. One of the Highlanders lay only a few feet away from Nithsdale, writhing in agony.

If you're not going to fight, you must at least try to help that man! Nithsdale thought. He closed his eyes, said a quick prayer, then hunched down and scrambled over to the fallen Scotsman.

The man lay in a pool of blood, his red eyes looking skyward, his teeth clenched. The cannonball had taken his arm off.

"Easy, lad," Nithsdale said.

He dropped his musket and, with some effort, managed to a scoop the screaming Highlander up over his shoulder. The two lumbered down the street and out of the line of fire, the Highlander cursing with every step.

By the time Nithsdale handed him off at the hospital tent, the Highlander was deathly pale. Nithsdale watched as others tried to stop the bleeding.

Poor devil. He ran into battle as I cowered behind a barrel, and yet he's the one who pays the price.

"Nithsdale!" His friend Lord Kenmure approached. "The British have us surrounded. There's no escape! We should have fled with the others when we still could."

Nithsdale didn't want to admit it, but perhaps Kenmure was right. The previous night, dozens of the Scottish rebels managed to silently slip out of town. A few of them had tried to convince Lord Nithsdale to join them.

"To stay is suicide," one said. "It will only end with your head on the chopping block."

Nithsdale had considered it. Though born in northern England, he had deep Scottish roots. On his twenty-first birthday, he had sworn his allegiance to the exiled Scottish king James—the same king the rebels were fighting to put back on the throne.

Feeling bound by honor and duty, Nithsdale chose to stay in the besieged town.

As he looked upon the dying Highlander, he couldn't help but regret that decision.

That night, Nithsdale and the rest of the leaders of the Jacobite forces met in a house. Jacobites were those who were fighting to get a Scottish king back on the throne. As the others talked about what to do, Lord Nithsdale peered out the window. Flames from the burning town licked the night sky. Beyond, camped on the hills just outside the city walls, was a sea of British tents with no end in sight. They clearly aimed to crush this rebellion now before the Scots made it farther south.

There must be at least three thousand redcoats out there, he thought. When the Jacobites had arrived in Preston, they numbered four thousand. Now they were less than half that.

"The British have the advantage," Nithsdale's friend Lord Derwentwater said. "It's over. We must surrender!"

"Aye!" Lord Kenmure said.

"Nithsdale," Thomas Forster, the general of the Jacobite forces, said from across the room. "What say you? Are you for surrendering, or shall we fight it out?"

Lord Nithsdale turned toward his fellow Jacobite leaders. He ran a hand through his black hair and took a deep breath.

"The British have the town surrounded," he said. "And we're heavily outnumbered. I see no other option but to surrender and throw ourselves at the mercy of King George."

"Never!" barked the Highlanders' leader. "You noblemen may do as you wish, but there'll be no surrender from us. Our men can crush these British, and to surrender in an effort to save one's own skin would not only be foolish but an act of cowardice. We'll have no part in it." He let the words sink in. "Good night, gentlemen."

The Highlanders turned and walked out of the room.

No one said a word for a good minute. Nithsdale and the others waited on their general to speak first.

"Farmers," Forster finally said with a sneer, speaking dismissively of the Highlanders. "Those cattlemen are obviously ignorant of the reality of our predicament."

But they are brave, Nithsdale thought. *They fought while I hid behind a barrel.*

"I agree with Nithsdale and Derwentwater," Forster said. "To stay and fight is suicide."

At seven o'clock the next morning, Nithsdale and the rest of the Jacobite leaders surrendered to the British.

THE JACOBITE UPRISINGS

From 1689 to 1746, a series of wars were waged between England and Scotland over who should be king.

Both countries shared a single ruler, but otherwise they were very different states—especially in terms of religion. Most Englishmen practiced a form of Christianity called Protestantism, while most of Scotland was Roman Catholic.

In 1688, when Nithsdale was twelve years old, James II was the king. James was born in Scotland and practiced Roman Catholicism. In 1707, England and Scotland became one kingdom known as Great Britain. The British parliament was Protestant, so they wanted to dethrone James. Parliament started a war called the Glorious Revolution, in which the British parliament asked Dutch Prince William III and Britain's William of Orange to be joint monarchs. The effort succeeded, and a new Protestant king was crowned.

Naturally, Scotland thought that wasn't fair, and had doubts that parliament's removal of a Scottish king was legal. So over the next fifty-plus years, the Jacobites and their sympathizers—like Nithsdale—fought to put the rightful Scottish heir back on the throne. They were called *Jacobites* because Jacob is Latin for James, the deposed king for whom they were fighting.

The war ended in 1746, when the Battle of Culloden proved to be the final Jacobite uprising, which the Jacobites lost. Prince Charles, the

Scottish heir who organized the failed revolt, ran off to France. He tried to get support for another revolt attempt while in Europe, but couldn't find any takers.

London, Mid-December–10:22 p.m.

Lord Nithsdale felt nauseated as the stagecoach careened down the cobblestone street. He and the two other lords sat in silence as they bumped up and down in their seats. What was there to say? The three men were being taken to the dreaded Tower of London, where they would be held until they were sentenced.

Nithsdale shifted his arms in an attempt to alleviate the pain in his wrists, which had been rubbed red and raw from the heavy iron shackles placed around them. He'd worn them often, having spent the past few weeks being moved to different jails around England.

Glancing through the barred windows, he caught a glimpse of the stone archway they were headed toward. Nithsdale recognized it from afar as the famous Temple Bar gate. Then something else caught his eye, something he'd never seen on his previous visits to London—there were strange sticks lined up along the top of the arch like porcupine quills.

Wait . . . what's on top of those poles?

When they neared the archway, he understood. These were sticks with severed heads stuck on the spiked tips. Some of the heads had their eyes open, staring blankly into the mist.

It feels as if I'm looking upon the Gates of Hell.

Nithsdale tried not to throw up as the carriage rolled through the gate. He thought about his wife, Winifred, and his son having to see his father's head on a spike and felt even more sick to his stomach.

After a few minutes, Nithsdale could smell the stink of the Thames River. He peered again through the barred windows of the stagecoach. Through the mist, he could see the foreboding stone wall of the Tower.

In the dark, it's like something out of a nightmare.

Armed guards kept a lookout from the top of the wall. Beyond it, Nithsdale could see the four spires of the Tower stretching high into the night, lights flickering in their windows. There was a cluster of other buildings around the main tower, making the entire compound seem like a small city within the city. Nithsdale had never been to the Tower on his previous trips into London—he'd seen it only from afar, in the daytime—but he knew it was to be feared. "The Bloody Tower," he'd heard it called. Men and women held there were brutally tortured within its chambers and, more often than not, barbarically executed.

As a lord rather than a commoner, Nithsdale knew he would be granted a stay in one of the better cells and would not be tortured. It didn't really matter, though. Noble or not, he would soon be dead just the same.

Inside the Tower walls, he saw prisoners—most of them Scottish Highlanders—shivering in the cold as they were led off to their cells, shuffling past a blood-stained chopping block.

Ready For More Risks?
Read the GREAT ESCAPES series!